NORTH HILL SCHOOL LIBRARY

P9-DNG-074

DISCARDED

4-15-2019

DATE DUE

Six Crows

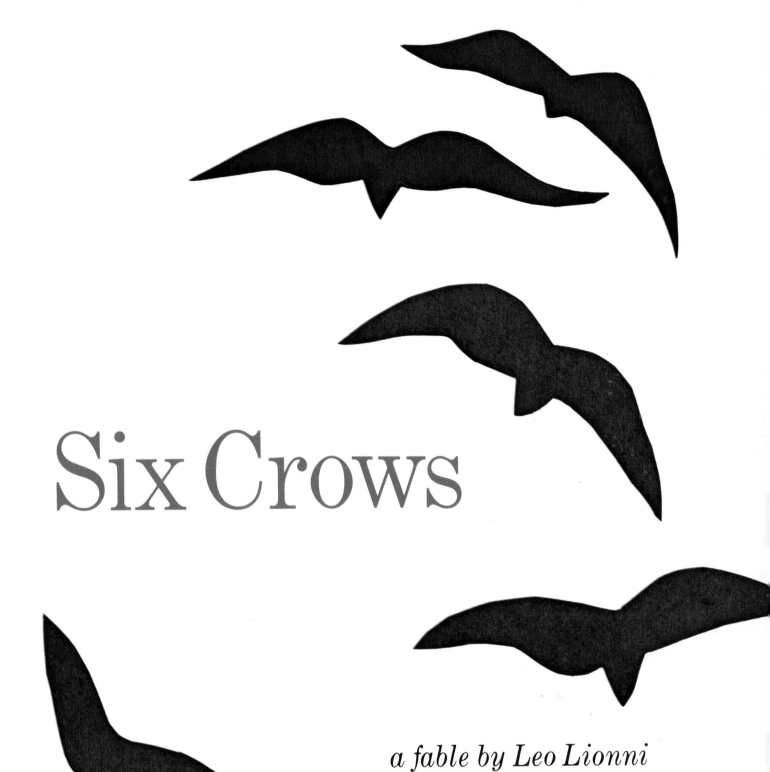

Six Crows

a fable by Leo Lionni

Alfred A. Knopf 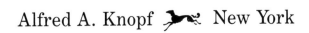 New York

In a peaceful valley at the foot of the Balabadur Hills a farmer cultivated a field of wheat. The soil was fertile and the spring rains had been gentle.

Life would have been good and happy were it not for six noisy crows who nested in a tree nearby.

Just when the wheat was about to ripen, the crows descended upon the field and pecked away at the tender grains.

The farmer tried to chase the crows from the field. But no sooner had he returned to his hut than they were back. In desperation he built a scarecrow.

When the crows saw it standing in the wheat, waving a
big stick, they were frightened. They huddled in their
tree and wondered what to do. "We must scare that
thing away!" they said. "But how?"

"Let's set the field on fire!" shouted a crow.

"But that would be the end of our wheat!" the others said.

There were many proposals. At last they agreed to make a ferocious kite. They gathered bark and dry leaves and made a fierce and very ugly bird.

The next morning they flew the kite over the field. The scarecrow didn't budge, but the farmer was very frightened. He ran into his hut and bolted the door tight. "I must build a scarier scarecrow," he said.

Soon a giant figure brandishing two swords stood in the wheat field. Its angry mouth seemed to grunt. "That should do it," said the farmer.

But when the crows saw the new menace, they gathered more bark and more leaves and built an even larger and more ferocious kite. They flew it over the field. Back and forth. The farmer was so scared that he didn't dare leave his hut.

From her nest in an old tree trunk an owl had been watching the goings on. She shook her head. "I don't know who is sillier, the farmer or the crows," she thought.

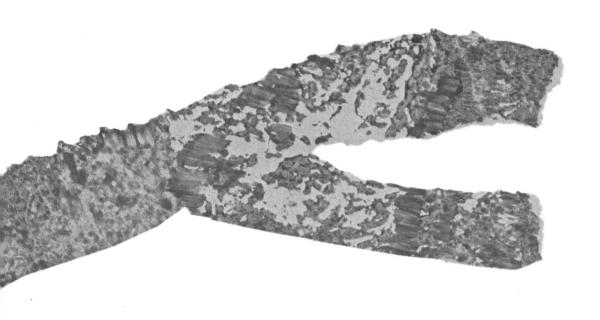

When she noticed that the wheat was wilting from neglect, she decided to talk to the farmer. "Why don't you make peace, you and the crows?" she said.

"It's too late now," said the farmer angrily.

"It's never too late to talk things over," said the owl.

Then she went to see the crows.

"What can we do now?" asked the crows, dismayed when they heard that the wheat crop was in danger.

"Go and talk things over," said the owl. "Words can do magic."

The crows and the farmer agreed to meet near the owl's nest. While the owl looked on they talked and talked. First in anger, then more reasonably, finally like old friends.

"I must confess that I missed your happy cackling," said the farmer.

"And we missed your wheat!" said the crows. Soon they were laughing together.

"We must thank the owl," said the farmer. "But where is she?"

Her nest was empty. They looked all over.

They went to the field. There stood the giant scarecrow, but something was different. The nasty grin had turned into a happy smile. The owl was perched on the giant's arm. "What happened?" they asked.

"Magic," she said.

Leo Lionni is internationally acclaimed as an artist, designer, sculptor, art director, and creator of animal fables for children. He is the recipient of the 1984 American Institute of Graphic Arts Gold Medal and is a four-time Caldecott Honor Book winner for *Inch by Inch, Swimmy, Alexander and the Wind-Up Mouse,* and *Frederick.* His picture books, noted for being both playful and serious, are distinguished by their graphic simplicity and brilliant use of collage.

Lionni was born in Amsterdam, Holland. He studied there, in Belgium, the U.S.A., Switzerland, and Italy, and received a Ph.D. in economics from the University of Genoa. In 1939 he came to this country with his wife, Nora, and their two sons. The Lionnis now divide their time between an apartment in the heart of New York City and a seventeenth-century farmhouse in Tuscany, Italy.

THIS IS A BORZOI BOOK PUBLISHED BY ALFRED A. KNOPF, INC.

Copyright © 1988 by Leo Lionni. All rights reserved under International and Pan-American Copyright Conventions. Published in the United States by Alfred A. Knopf, Inc., New York, and simultaneously in Canada by Random House of Canada Limited, Toronto. Distributed by Random House, Inc., New York. Manufactured in the United States of America 10 9 8 7 6 5 4 3 2 1

Library of Congress Cataloging-in-Publication Data: Lionni, Leo, 1910— . Six crows. Summary: An owl helps a farmer and some crows reach a compromise over the rights to the wheat crop. [1. Farm life—Fiction] I. Title. PZ7.L6634Si 1988 [E] 87-3141 ISBN 0-394-89572-X ISBN 0-394-99572-4 (lib. bdg.)